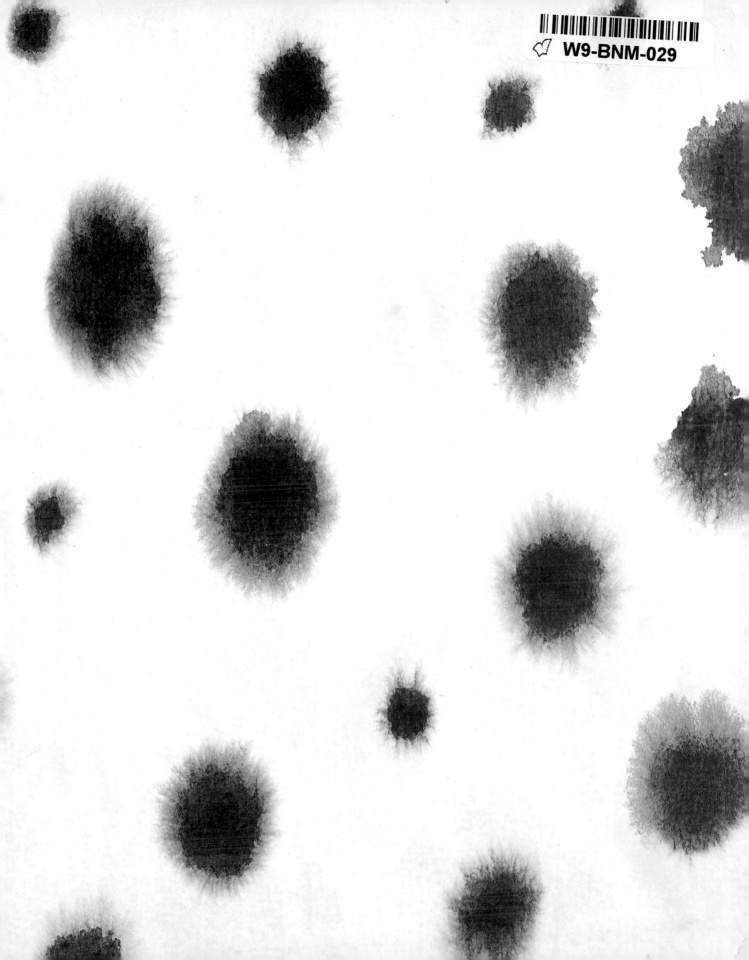

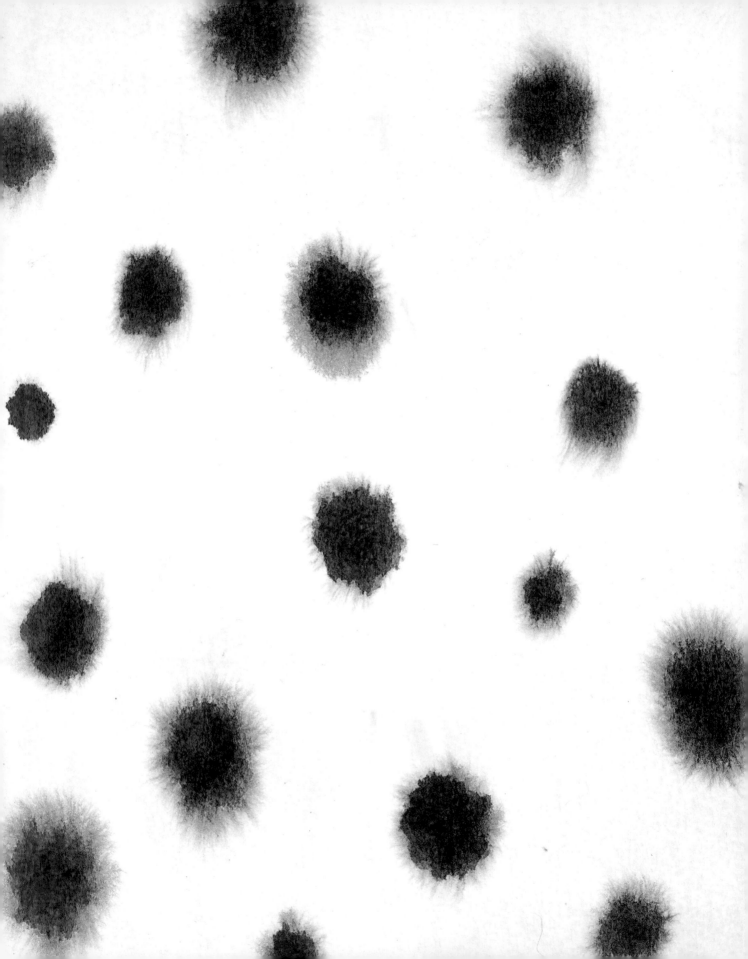

OSCAR'S
SPOTS

OSCAR'S SPOTS

JANET ROBERTSON

Troll Medallion

Oscar was fed up. "I hate the way I look,"
he grumbled. "I'm bored with my leopard fur.

"Every time I look in the mirror,
I see spots before my eyes."

Dad was in the kitchen.

"I want to change my image," said Oscar.
"A leopard can't change his spots," Dad laughed.
"But you could try a disguise."

So Oscar found some old
clothes in the toy box . . .

and put them on . . .

"Nobody will recognize me now," he said.

Kathryn and Matthew came to play.

"Hello Oscar," they said.

"How did you know it was me?" sighed Oscar.

"Your spots gave you away," said Matthew.

"A leopard can't change his spots, you know,"
said Kathryn.

"Grrrr," growled Oscar.

Kathryn and Matthew thought about
how they could change Oscar's spots. They used
some make-up . . . it made Oscar sneeze . . .

Oscar's big sister came in. "Have you seen
my make-up?" Brenda asked.

Brenda was very upset. Dad was angry.
''Go and wash that mess off at once,'' he said in a
stern voice.

Oscar and his friends went shopping for something that would change Oscar's image.

But they couldn't agree on a single thing.

On the way home, they went down a street they had never seen before.

One shop in particular caught Oscar's eye.

"That's the answer!" yelled Oscar. "Magic will change my spots! Let's go inside!"

"I hope you know what you're doing," said Kathryn.

Mr. Wobble was behind the counter.
"Hello," he said.
"Can I help you?"

Marvo!

"I'm bored with my spots,"
said Oscar.
"Can you do a special spell for me,
please?"

"Are you sure that's what you want?" asked Mr. Wobble.
"You know what they say—a leopard can't change his spots."

"Can't you magic them away?" asked Oscar.
"I'd give anything to be a spotless leopard."

"Well, I'll see what I can do," said Mr. Wobble, looking in his book of spells and potions.

He soon found the spell he wanted. He took different things from his shelves and began his magic spell . . .

He measured . . .

and mixed . . .

and shook . . .

and stirred . . .

until all the ingredients were blended together.

Then Mr. Wobble poured the magic potion into a small blue bottle.

"This should do the trick," he said, writing out a label. "Use it like shampoo. Be sure to follow the instructions very carefully indeed."

Oscar, Kathryn and Matthew raced home. Oscar couldn't wait to get started! But Oscar was in such a hurry that he forgot to read the instructions and poured the *whole bottle* of magic shampoo over himself.

"Oh dear," said Kathryn. "I think you've used too much." Kathryn was right. The label on the bottle said: USE SPARINGLY OR ELSE.

But Oscar didn't care, because his spots were washing away like dirt, right down the drain!

What a difference! Not a spot in sight!
Oscar was so pleased with his new image, he
decided to go for a walk.

Nobody recognized him.
Even his own sister and her boyfriend
walked straight past.
"Who says a leopard can't change his spots,"
said Oscar smugly.

But then, all of a sudden, Oscar began to feel very odd. His body was tingling! From the tops of his ears to the tip of his tail, Oscar's fur was standing up on end!

"What's happening?" he squealed. Kathryn and Matthew didn't answer. They were too busy watching Oscar's fur start to change, right before their eyes . . .

"You definitely used too much shampoo,"
said Matthew.

"Help!" cried Oscar, and he ran as fast as he
could back to the magic shop with Kathryn
and Matthew trailing behind.

"Oh Mr. Wobble!" sobbed Oscar. "I've changed my mind. Please magic me back to the way I was!"

Mr. Wobble agreed to help. Kathryn and Matthew brought him his spell book.

Luckily for Oscar, Mr. Wobble found some magic paint, and he very carefully painted Oscar's spots back on. It took a long time and Oscar had to stand very still.

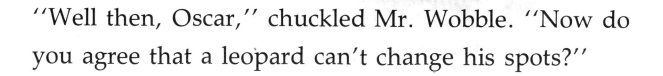

"Well then, Oscar," chuckled Mr. Wobble. "Now do you agree that a leopard can't change his spots?"

"Oh yes," said Oscar. "I only wanted to be unusual, but I guess I'll settle for the way I am. It's lovely to be myself again."

Mr. Wobble, Kathryn and Matthew chuckled to themselves and waited for the paint to dry.

Don't you agree that Oscar is now a very unusual leopard? Very unusual indeed!

Published by Troll Associates, Inc.

First published by Blackie Children's Books, Penguin Books Ltd.
27 Wrights Lane, London W8 5TZ England.

Published in the United States in hardcover by BridgeWater Books.

Printed in the United States of America.

10 9 8 7 6 5 4 3 2 1

Library of Congress Cataloging-in-Publication Data

Robertson, Janet.
    Oscar's spots / by Janet Robertson.
        p.   cm.
    Summary: After visiting a magician, a young leopard who had been
unhappy with his appearance learns to like the way he looks.
    ISBN 0-8167-3133-0 (lib. bdg.)   ISBN 0-8167-3134-9 (pbk.)
  [1. Leopard—Fiction.   2. Self-acceptance—Fiction.   2. Magic—
Fiction.]   I. Title.
PZ7.R5455Os   1993
[E]—dc20   93-22199

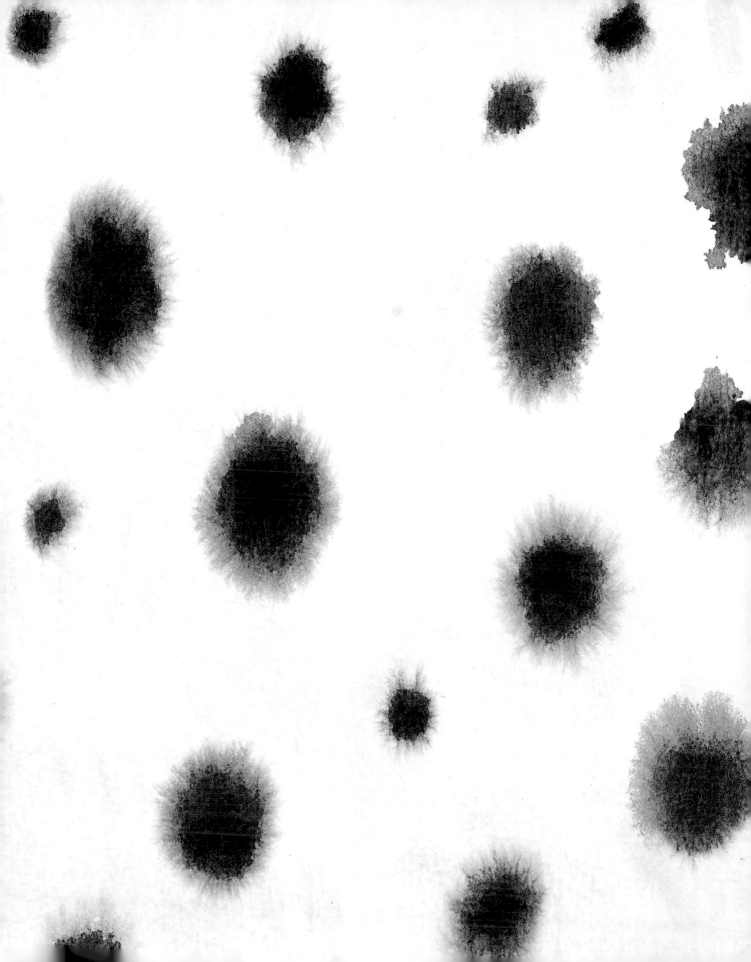

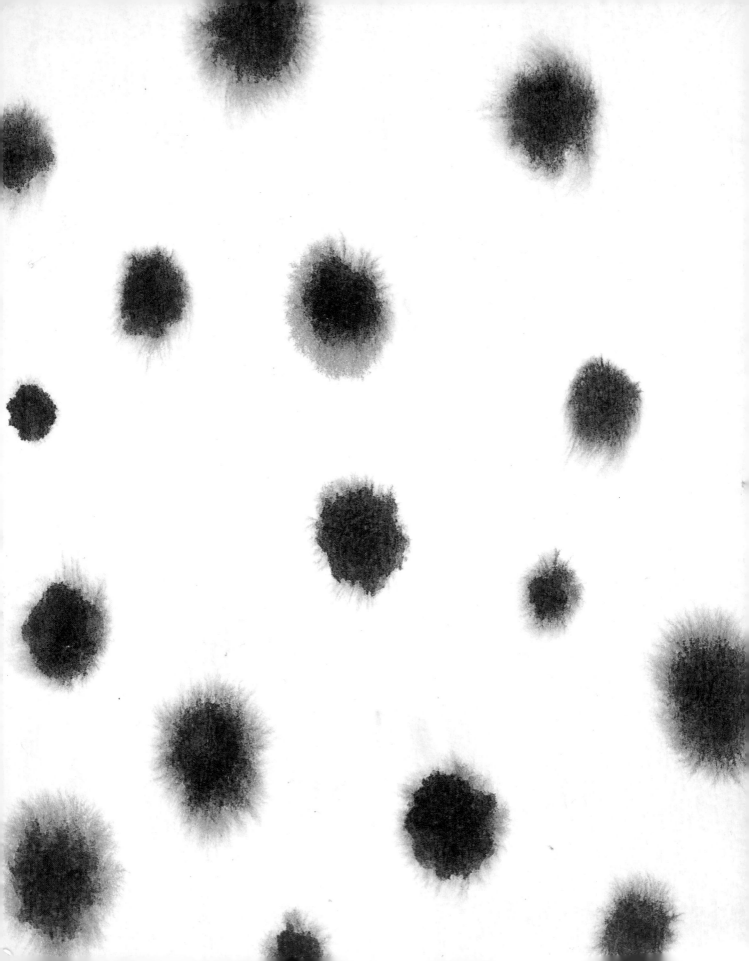